# TRANSFORMERS
## DARK OF THE MOON
# FOUNDATION

## VOLUME 4


STORY BY JOHN BARBER

ART BY ANDREW GRIFFITH



COLORS BY PRISCILLA TRAMONTANO

LETTERS BY CHRIS MOWRY AND SHAWN LEE

SERIES ASSISTANT EDITOR CARLOS GUZMAN

SERIES EDITOR ANDY SCHMIDT

COLLECTION EDITOR JUSTIN EISINGER

COLLECTION DESIGNER SHAWN LEE

Licensed By:

GM Hasbro Paramount IDW Spotlight

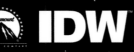

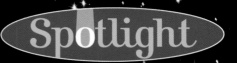

**visit us at www.abdopublishing.com**

Reinforced library bound edition published in 2012 by Spotlight,
a division of the ABDO Group, PO Box 398166, Minneapolis, MN 55439.
Spotlight produces high-quality reinforced library bound editions for schools and
libraries. Published by agreement with IDW Publishing. www.idwpublishing.com

Printed in the United States of America, North Mankato, Minnesota.
102011
012012
♻ This book contains at least 10% recycled materials.

**Library of Congress Cataloging-in-Publication Data**

Barber, John, 1976-
  Transformers, dark of the moon movie prequel / story by John Barber ; art by
Andrew Griffith ; colors by Priscilla Tramontano ; letters by Chris Mowry.
    p. cm. -- (Dark of the moon: foundation ; v. 4)
  ISBN 978-1-59961-971-2 (volume 1) -- ISBN 978-1-59961-972-9 (volume 2) --
ISBN 978-1-59961-973-6 (volume 3) -- ISBN 978-1-59961-974-3 (volume 4)
  1. Graphic novels. I. Griffith, Andrew, 1976- ill. II. Transformers, dark of the moon
(Motion picture) III. Title. IV. Title: Dark of the moon movie prequel.
  PZ7.7.B35Tr 2012
  741.5'973--dc23
                          2011029052

All Spotlight books are reinforced library binding
and manufactured in the United States of America.

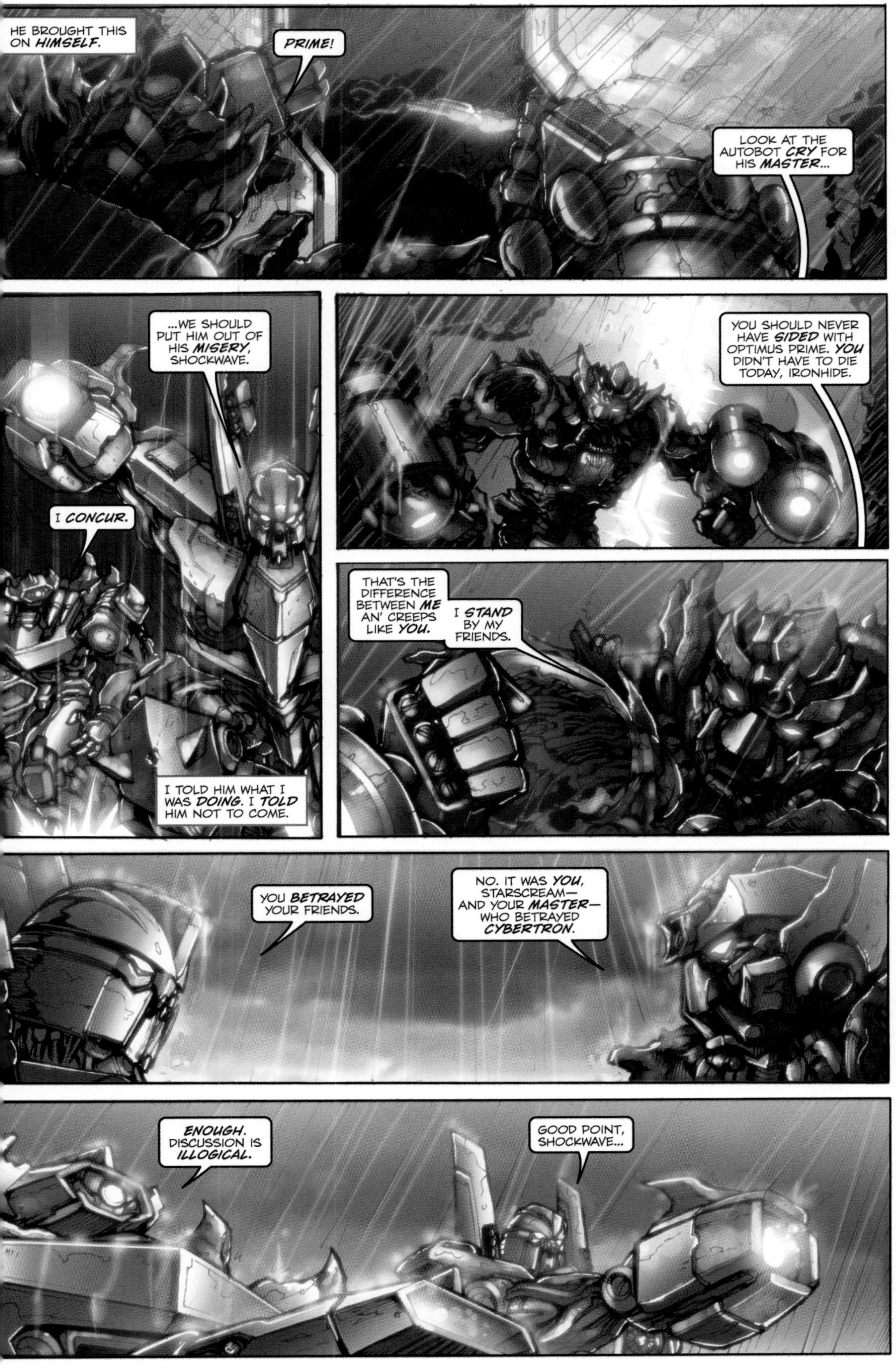
HE BROUGHT THIS ON HIMSELF.
PRIME!
LOOK AT THE AUTOBOT CRY FOR HIS MASTER...
...WE SHOULD PUT HIM OUT OF HIS MISERY, SHOCKWAVE.
I CONCUR.
I TOLD HIM WHAT I WAS DOING. I TOLD HIM NOT TO COME.
YOU SHOULD NEVER HAVE SIDED WITH OPTIMUS PRIME. YOU DIDN'T HAVE TO DIE TODAY, IRONHIDE.
THAT'S THE DIFFERENCE BETWEEN ME AN' CREEPS LIKE YOU.
I STAND BY MY FRIENDS.
YOU BETRAYED YOUR FRIENDS.
NO. IT WAS YOU, STARSCREAM—AND YOUR MASTER—WHO BETRAYED CYBERTRON.
ENOUGH. DISCUSSION IS ILLOGICAL.
GOOD POINT, SHOCKWAVE...

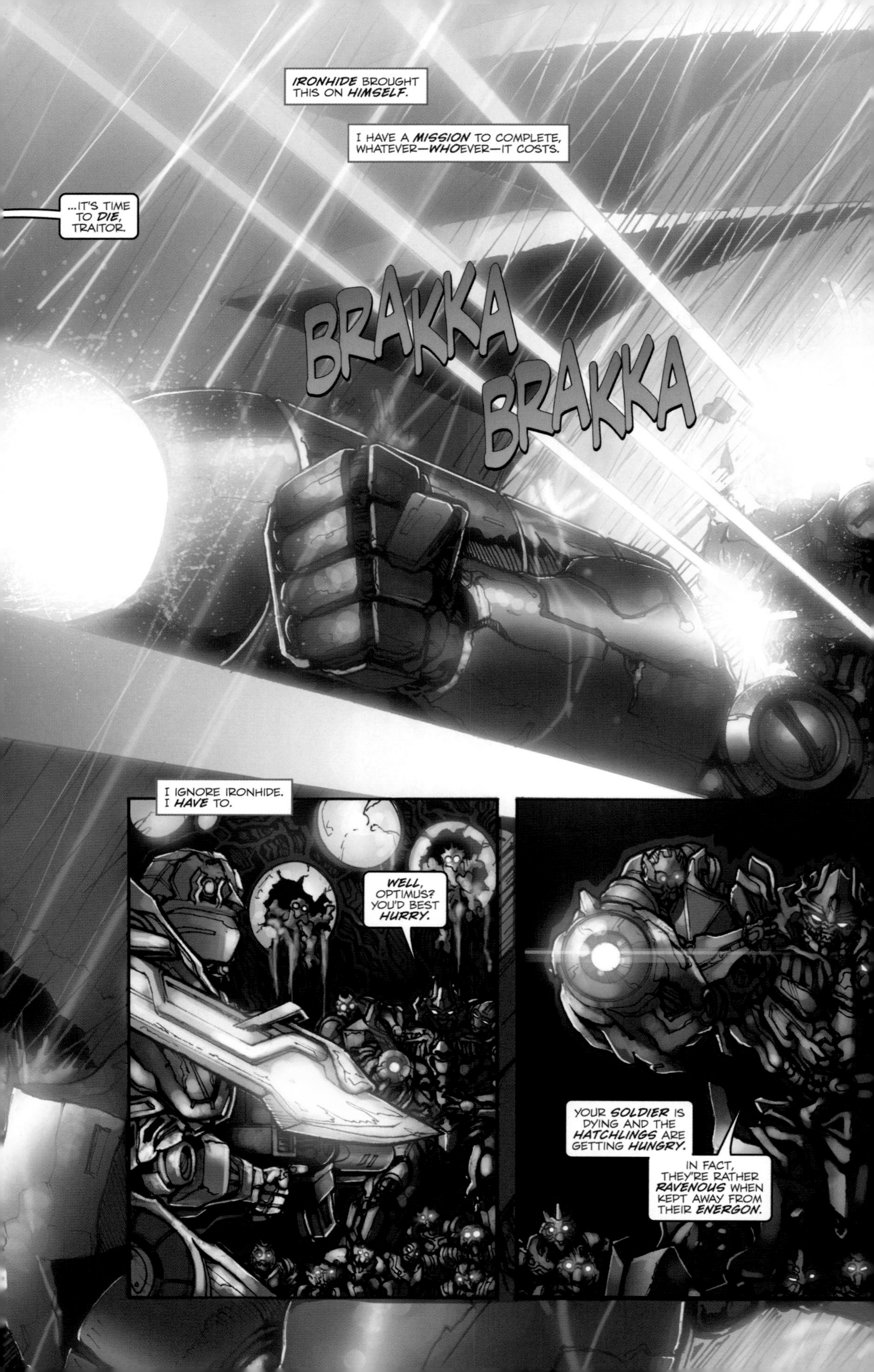
IRONHIDE BROUGHT THIS ON HIMSELF.
I HAVE A MISSION TO COMPLETE, WHATEVER—WHOEVER—IT COSTS.
...IT'S TIME TO DIE, TRAITOR.
BRAKKA BRAKKA
I IGNORE IRONHIDE. I HAVE TO.
WELL, OPTIMUS? YOU'D BEST HURRY.
YOUR SOLDIER IS DYING AND THE HATCHLINGS ARE GETTING HUNGRY.
IN FACT, THEY'RE RATHER RAVENOUS WHEN KEPT AWAY FROM THEIR ENERGON.

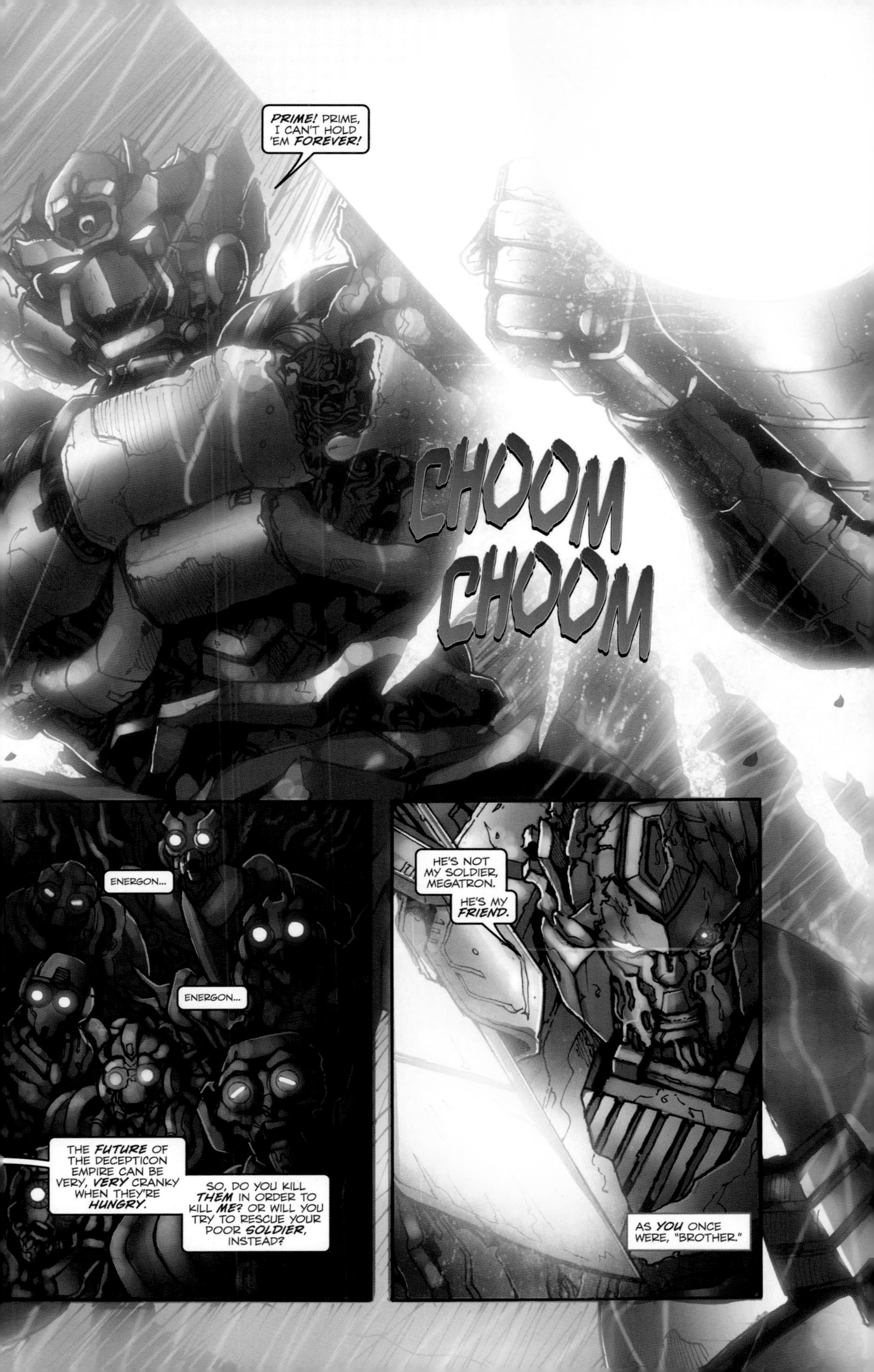

PRIME! PRIME, I CAN'T HOLD 'EM FOREVER!
CHOOM
CHOOM
ENERGON...
ENERGON...
THE FUTURE OF THE DECEPTICON EMPIRE CAN BE VERY, VERY CRANKY WHEN THEY'RE HUNGRY.
SO, DO YOU KILL THEM IN ORDER TO KILL ME? OR WILL YOU TRY TO RESCUE YOUR POOR SOLDIER, INSTEAD?
HE'S NOT MY SOLDIER, MEGATRON.
HE'S MY FRIEND.
AS YOU ONCE WERE, "BROTHER."

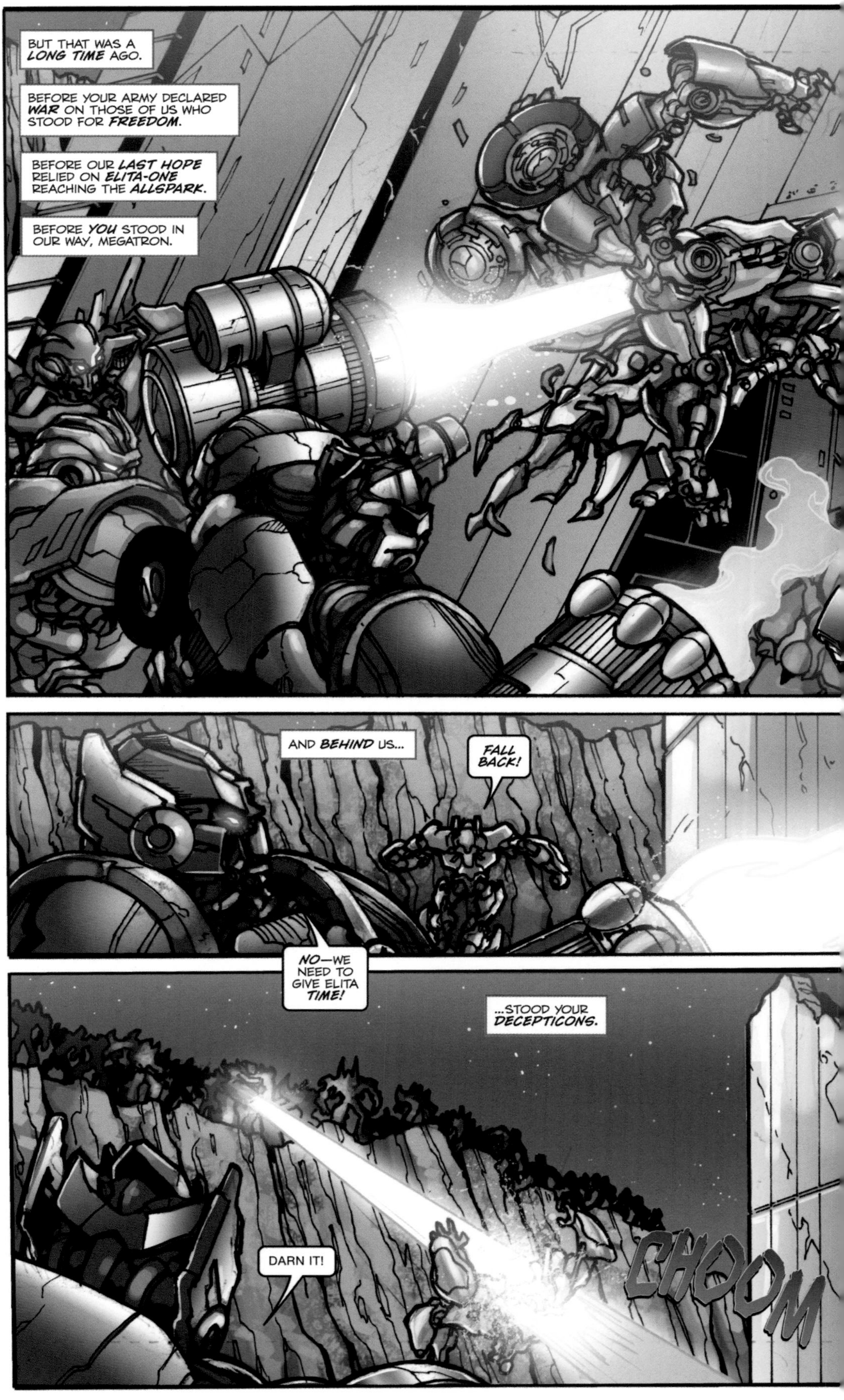

BUT THAT WAS A LONG TIME AGO.
BEFORE YOUR ARMY DECLARED WAR ON THOSE OF US WHO STOOD FOR FREEDOM.
BEFORE OUR LAST HOPE RELIED ON ELITA-ONE REACHING THE ALLSPARK.
BEFORE YOU STOOD IN OUR WAY, MEGATRON.
AND BEHIND US...
FALL BACK!
NO—WE NEED TO GIVE ELITA TIME!
...STOOD YOUR DECEPTICONS.
DARN IT!
CHOOM

MAKE YOUR PEACE WITH PRIMUS, AUTOBOTS— FOR TONIGHT YOU DIE!
THERE IS NOWHERE TO RUN, AUTOBOTS.
WAIT... THE FEMALES!
CHOOM
IS THIS GONNA WORK, CHROMIA?
AS LONG AS THEY DIDN'T CHANGE THE ACCESS CODES...
BLEEP
...YEAH, WE'RE IN.

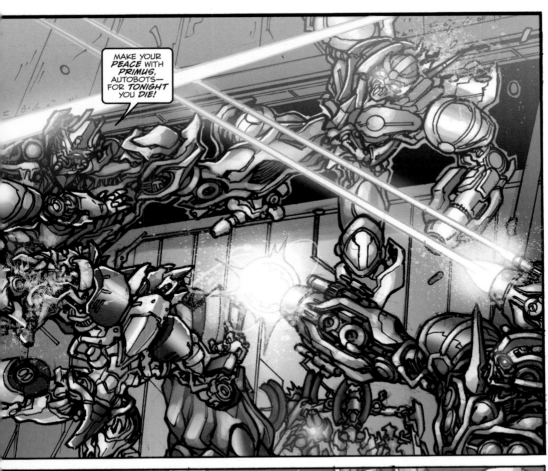

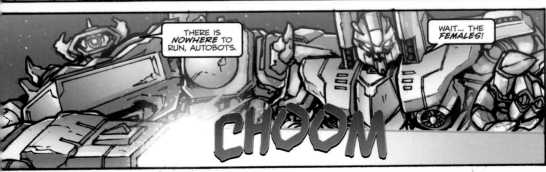

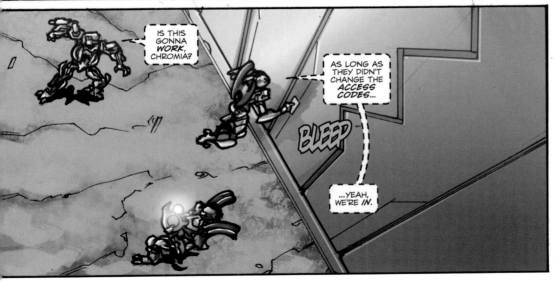

MEGATRON! THE DOOR!
I SEE THEM, STARSCREAM. ENOUGH OF THIS NONSENSE. DECEPTICONS—
—EXTERMINATE THE AUTOBOTS.
AIIIEEE!
SHZZ-RAKK
ELITA, HURRY!
I DON'T KNOW HOW LONG ARCEE AND I WILL BE ABLE TO HOLD THEM OFF!
HOW ODD...
...I KNOW EXACTLY HOW LONG.
KA-KROOM
CHA-KRAMM

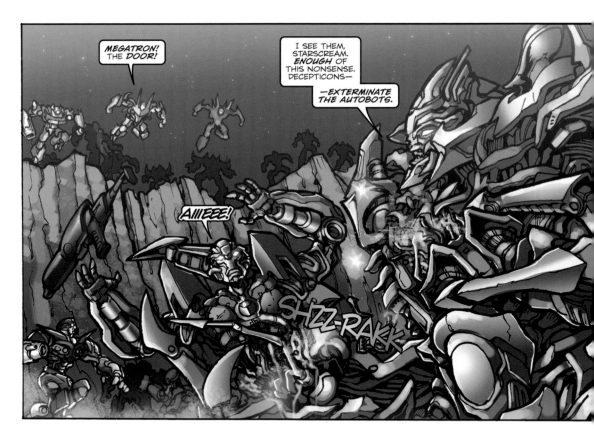

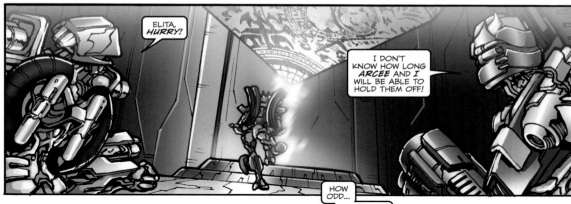

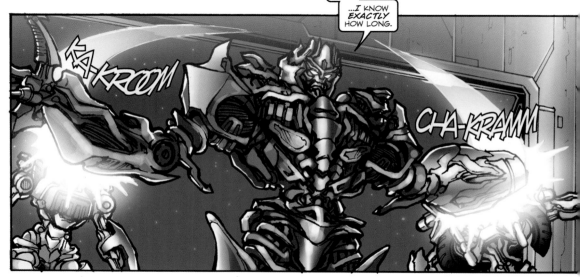

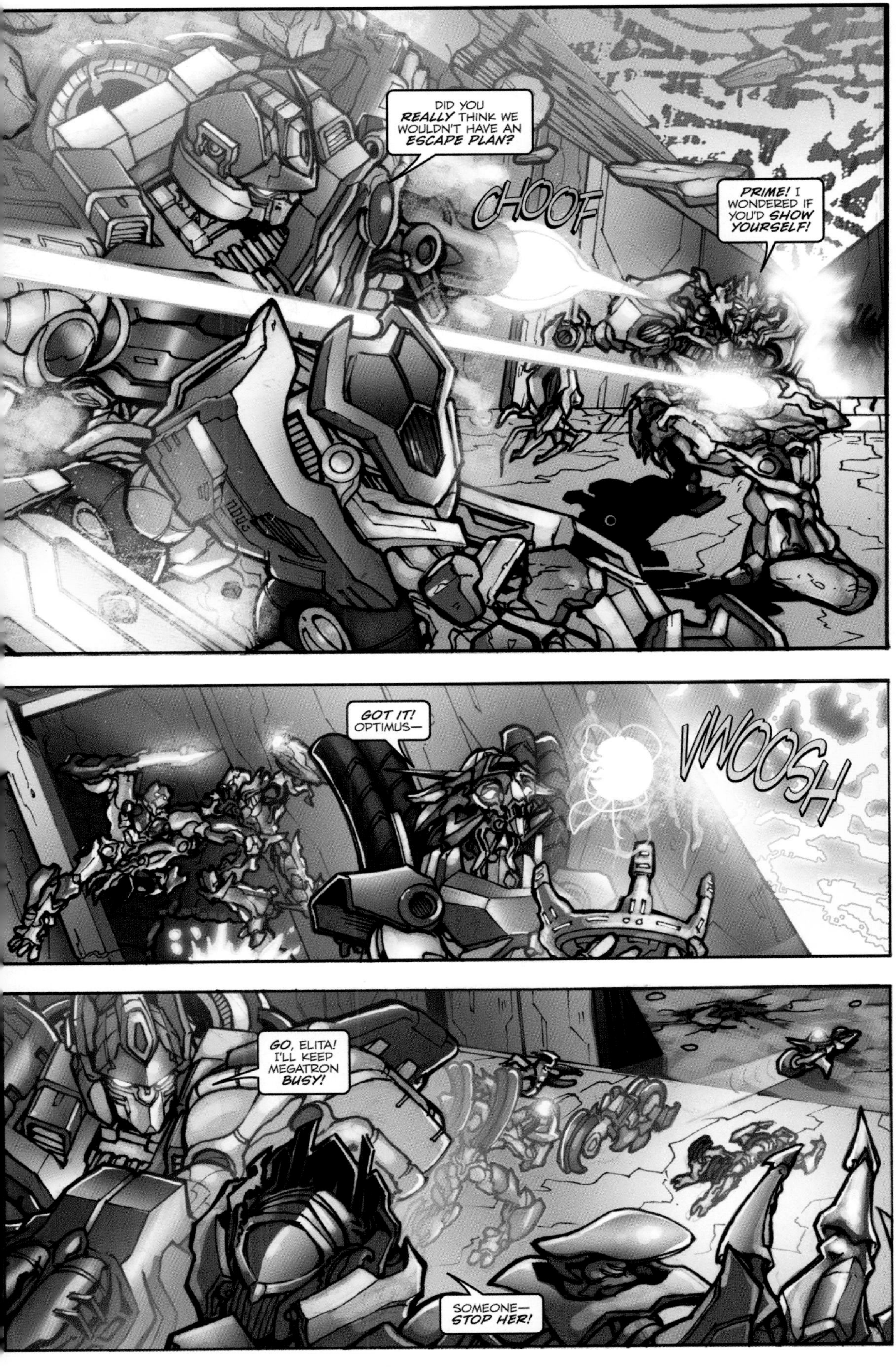

DID YOU REALLY THINK WE WOULDN'T HAVE AN ESCAPE PLAN?
CHOOF
PRIME! I WONDERED IF YOU'D SHOW YOURSELF!
GOT IT! OPTIMUS—
VWOOSH
GO, ELITA! I'LL KEEP MEGATRON BUSY!
SOMEONE— STOP HER!

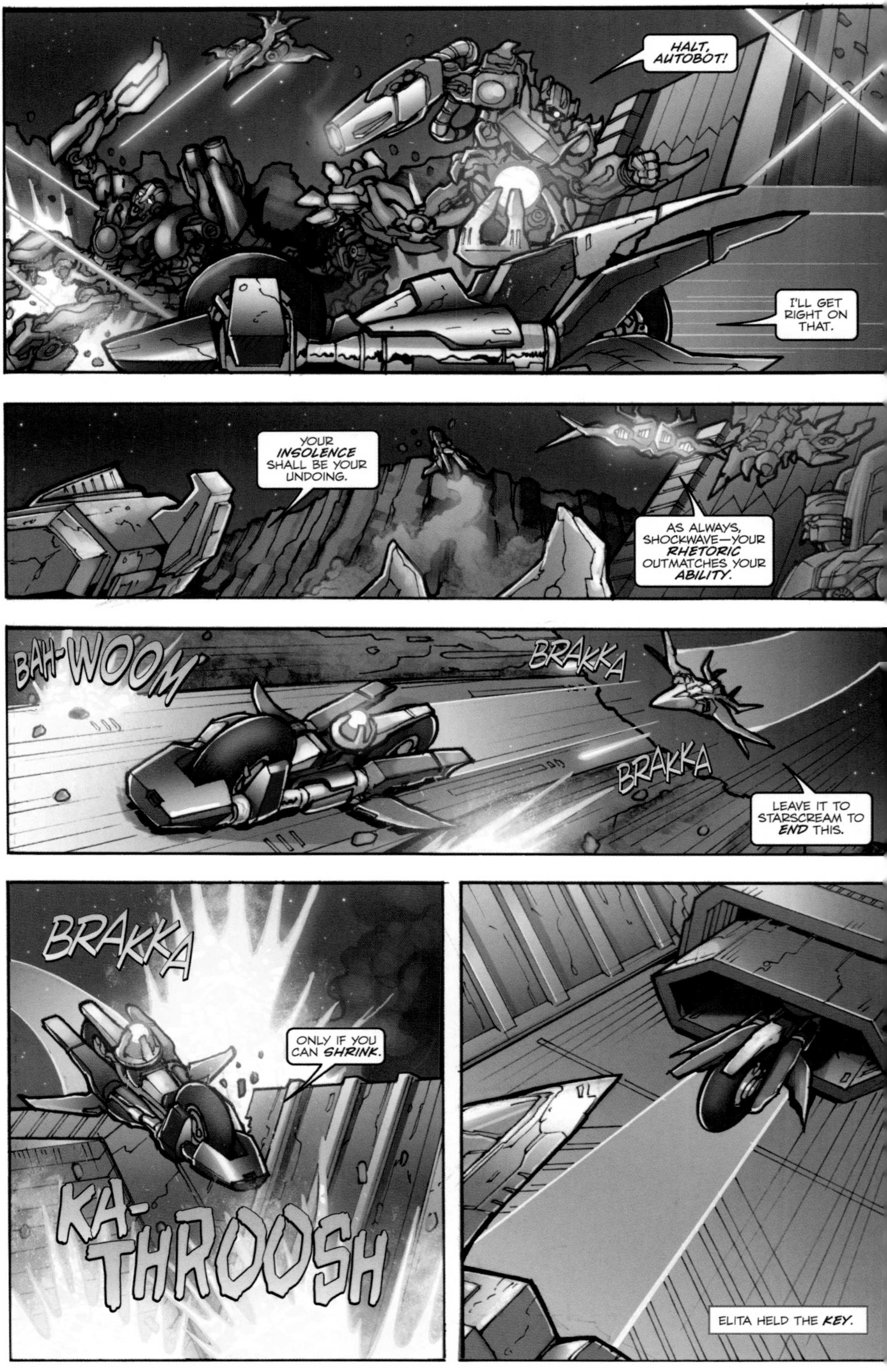
HALT, AUTOBOT!
I'LL GET RIGHT ON THAT.
YOUR INSOLENCE SHALL BE YOUR UNDOING.
AS ALWAYS, SHOCKWAVE—YOUR RHETORIC OUTMATCHES YOUR ABILITY.
BAH-WOOM
BRAKKA
BRAKKA
LEAVE IT TO STARSCREAM TO END THIS.
BRAKKA
ONLY IF YOU CAN SHRINK.
KA-THROOSH
ELITA HELD THE KEY.

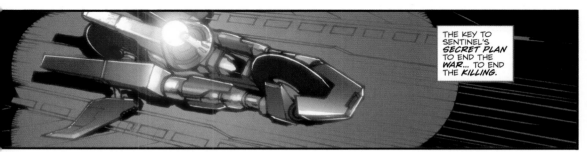

THE KEY TO SENTINEL'S *SECRET PLAN* TO END THE *WAR*... TO END THE *KILLING*.

*TWO SHIPS* HAD BEEN PREPARED TO CARRY US TO A *NEW FUTURE*.

STARSCREAM'S ON MY TRAIL—I TRIED TO *LOSE* HIM, BUT—

BUT HE'S *STARSCREAM*. WE'LL HAVE TO MOVE FAST.

WILL PILOT THE ...RK TO OPTIMUS ...ND THE OTHERS ...T THE TEMPLE.

WHEELJACK—TAKE THE SECOND CRAFT TO *TYGER PAX* AND GET THE *REST* OF THE AUTOBOTS.

BUT, SENTINEL...

WHAT WOULD YOU *GIVE* TO SAVE OUR *WORLD*?

*ANYTHING.* YOU *KNOW* THAT.

THEN DO *THIS* FOR ME.

DO THIS AND THE WAR'S *OVER*, OLD FRIEND.

I HOPE SENTINEL IS *RIGHT*.

HE USUALLY *IS*. AND *WE'D* BETTER MOVE.

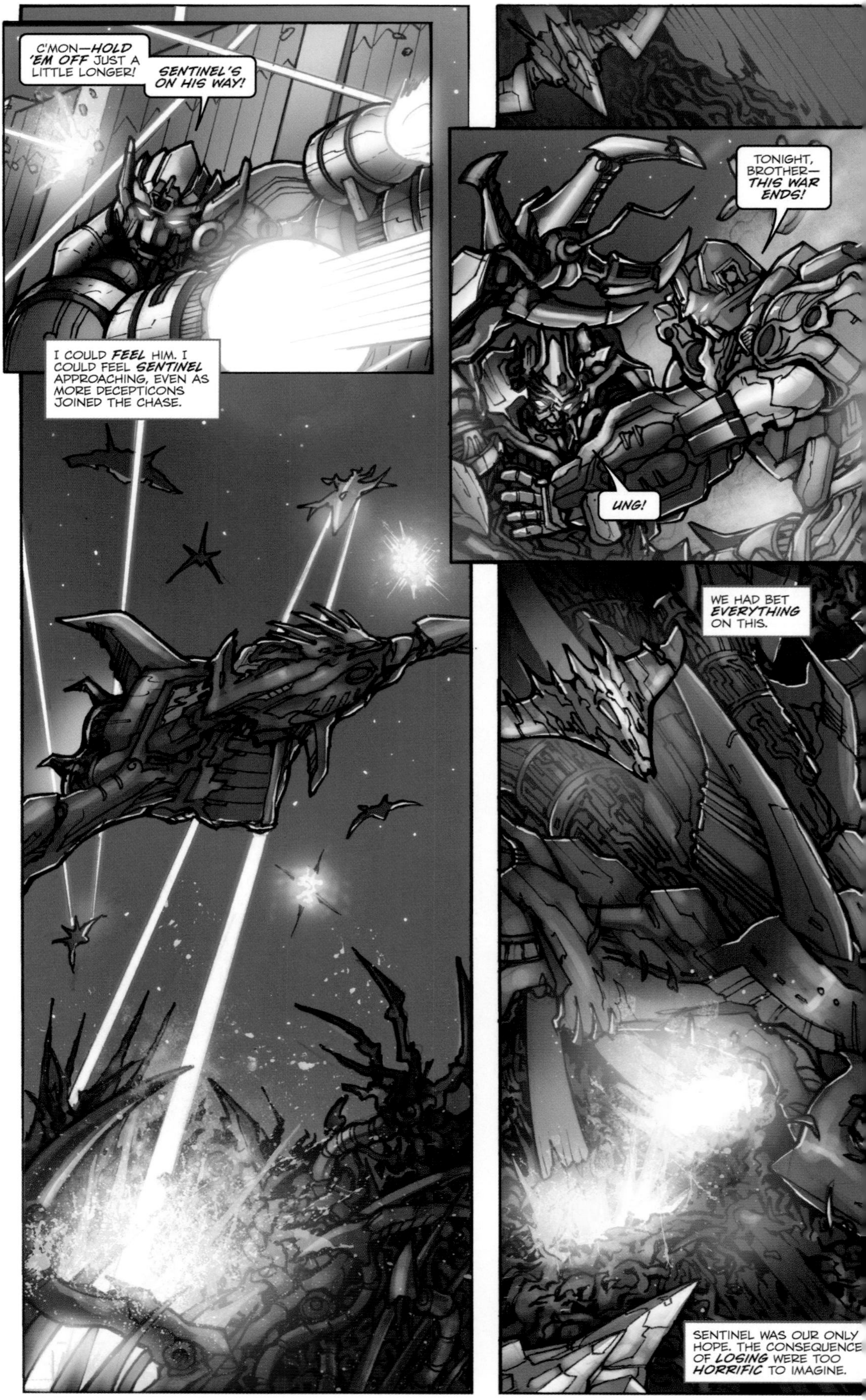
C'MON—HOLD 'EM OFF JUST A LITTLE LONGER!
SENTINEL'S ON HIS WAY!
I COULD FEEL HIM. I COULD FEEL SENTINEL APPROACHING, EVEN AS MORE DECEPTICONS JOINED THE CHASE.
TONIGHT, BROTHER— THIS WAR ENDS!
UNG!
WE HAD BET EVERYTHING ON THIS.
SENTINEL WAS OUR ONLY HOPE. THE CONSEQUENCE OF LOSING WERE TOO HORRIFIC TO IMAGINE.

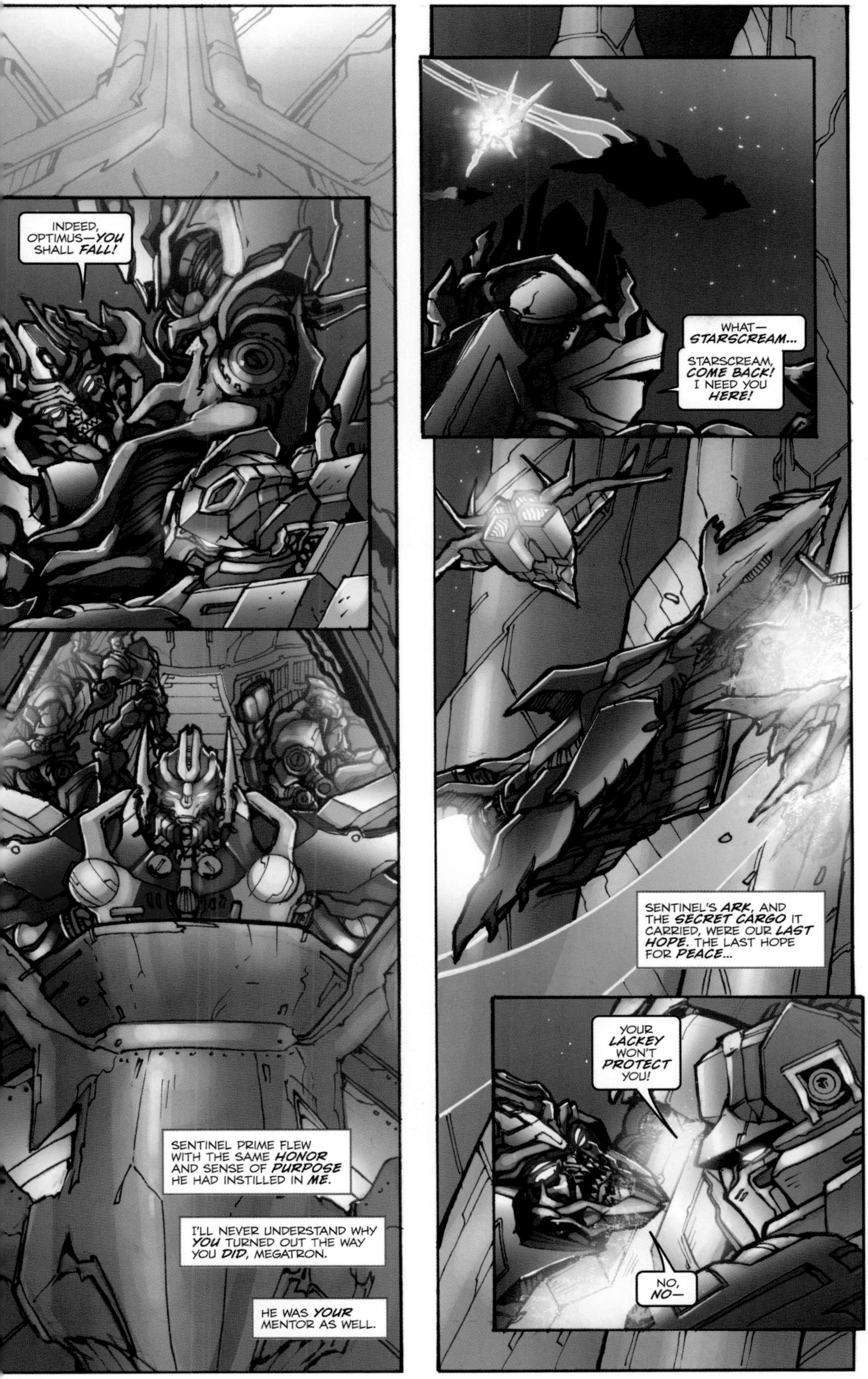
INDEED, OPTIMUS—YOU SHALL FALL!
SENTINEL PRIME FLEW WITH THE SAME HONOR AND SENSE OF PURPOSE HE HAD INSTILLED IN ME.
I'LL NEVER UNDERSTAND WHY YOU TURNED OUT THE WAY YOU DID, MEGATRON.
HE WAS YOUR MENTOR AS WELL.
WHAT— STARSCREAM...
STARSCREAM, COME BACK! I NEED YOU HERE!
SENTINEL'S ARK, AND THE SECRET CARGO IT CARRIED, WERE OUR LAST HOPE. THE LAST HOPE FOR PEACE...
YOUR LACKEY WON'T PROTECT YOU!
NO, NO—

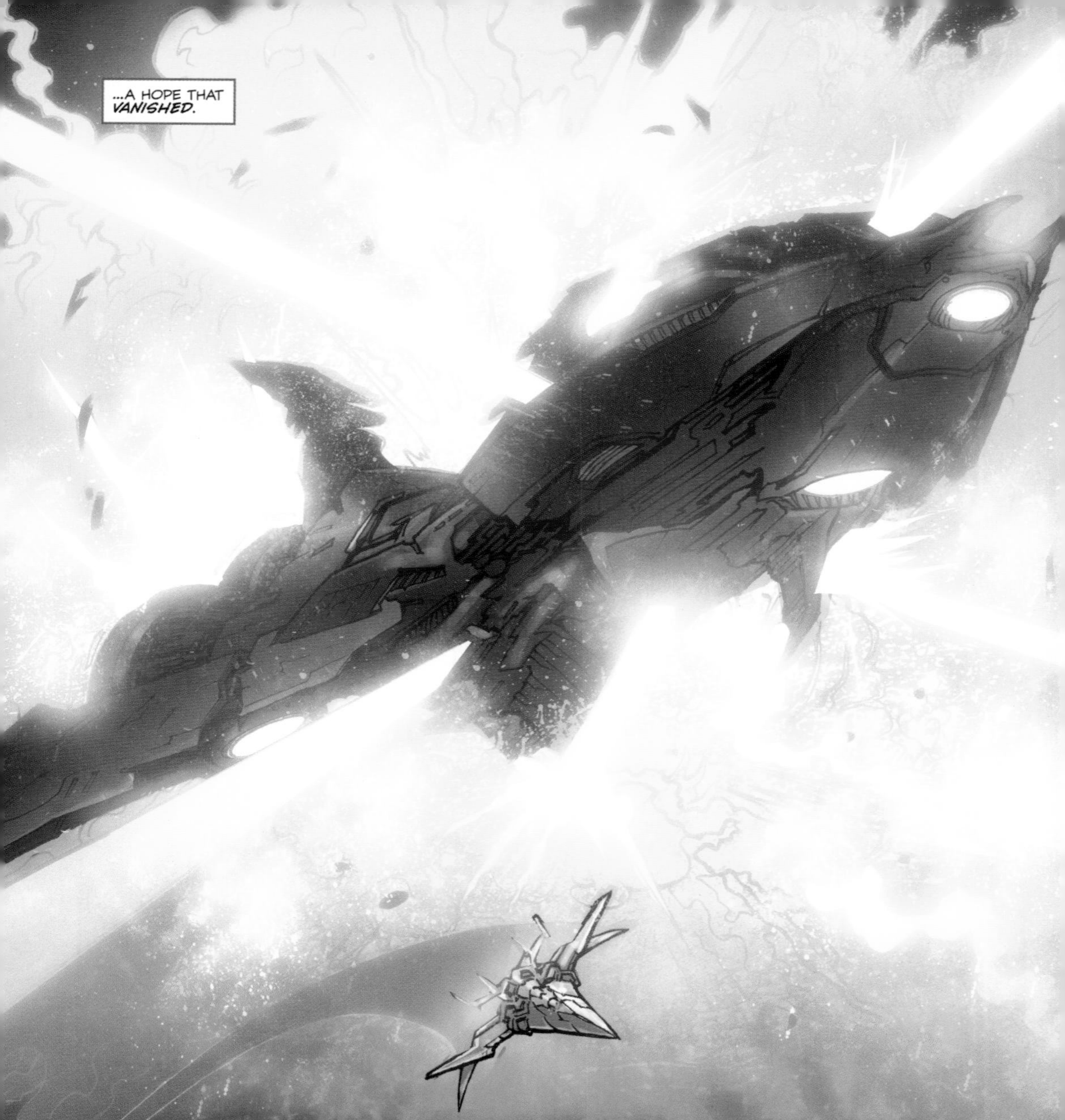
...A HOPE THAT VANISHED.

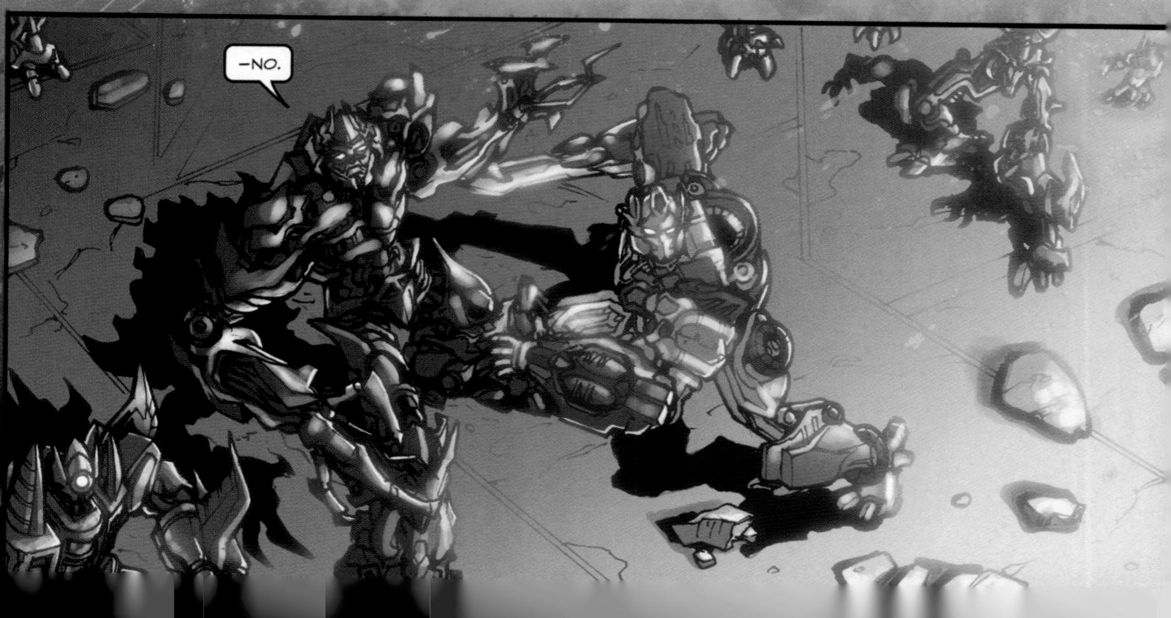
-NO.

IT... CAN'T BE.

NOOOOOO!

AUTOBOTS— FOLLOW PRIME!

FALL BACK AND LOOK FOR SURVIVORS!

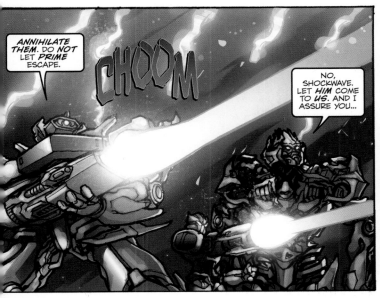

ANNIHILATE THEM. DO NOT LET PRIME ESCAPE.

CHOOM

NO, SHOCKWAVE. LET HIM COME TO US. AND I ASSURE YOU...

...HE WILL.

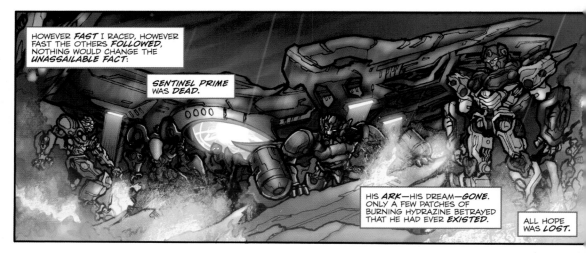

HOWEVER *FAST* I RACED, HOWEVER FAST THE OTHERS *FOLLOWED*, NOTHING WOULD CHANGE THE *UNASSAILABLE FACT:*

SENTINEL PRIME WAS *DEAD.*

HIS *ARK*—HIS DREAM—*GONE.* ONLY A FEW PATCHES OF BURNING HYDRAZINE BETRAYED THAT HE HAD EVER *EXISTED.*

ALL HOPE WAS *LOST.*

I WAS *WRONG.*

MEGATRON'S EVIL CAN'T BE *ALLOWED* TO *SURVIVE.*

REGROUP IN *TYGER PAX.* EVERYONE, GET ONBOARD THE... THE *REMAINING ARK.*

WHEELJACK— I HAVE A *MISSION* FOR YOU...

...BUT ONCE I GIVE THE SOLDIERS THEIR ORDERS, THERE'S SOMETHING I HAVE TO DO.

OPTIMUS—I KNOW WHAT *SENTINEL* MEANT TO YOU. YOU NEED YOUR *FRIENDS* NOW.

LEAVE ME ALONE, ELITA. ALL I NEED IS MEGATRON—

—DEAD.

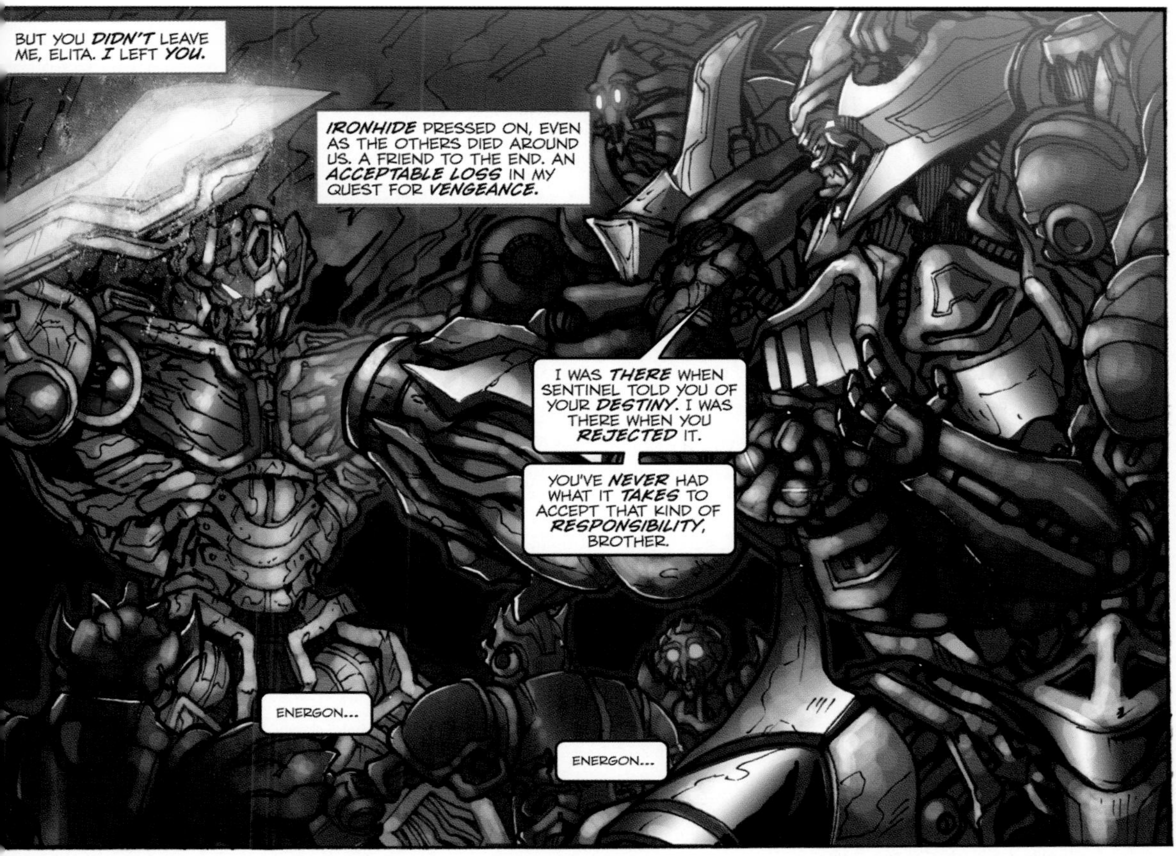
BUT YOU DIDN'T LEAVE ME, ELITA. I LEFT YOU.
IRONHIDE PRESSED ON, EVEN AS THE OTHERS DIED AROUND US. A FRIEND TO THE END. AN ACCEPTABLE LOSS IN MY QUEST FOR VENGEANCE.
I WAS THERE WHEN SENTINEL TOLD YOU OF YOUR DESTINY. I WAS THERE WHEN YOU REJECTED IT.
YOU'VE NEVER HAD WHAT IT TAKES TO ACCEPT THAT KIND OF RESPONSIBILITY, BROTHER.
ENERGON...
ENERGON...

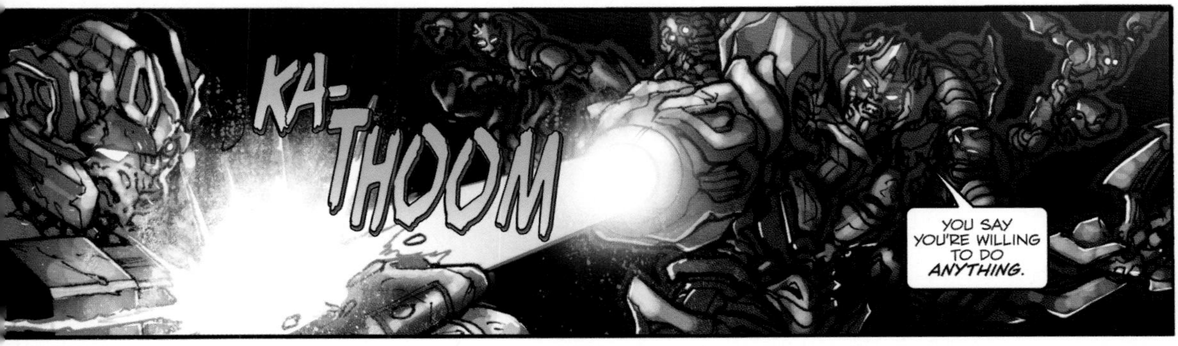
KA-THOOM
YOU SAY YOU'RE WILLING TO DO ANYTHING.

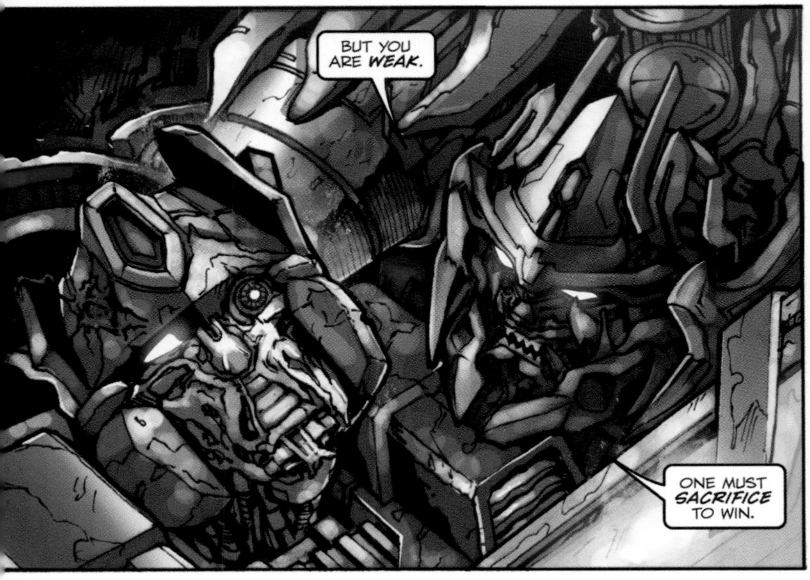
BUT YOU ARE WEAK.
ONE MUST SACRIFICE TO WIN.

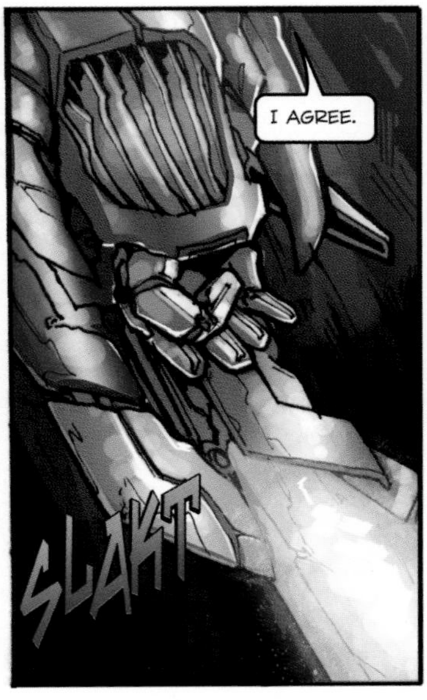
I AGREE.
SLAKT

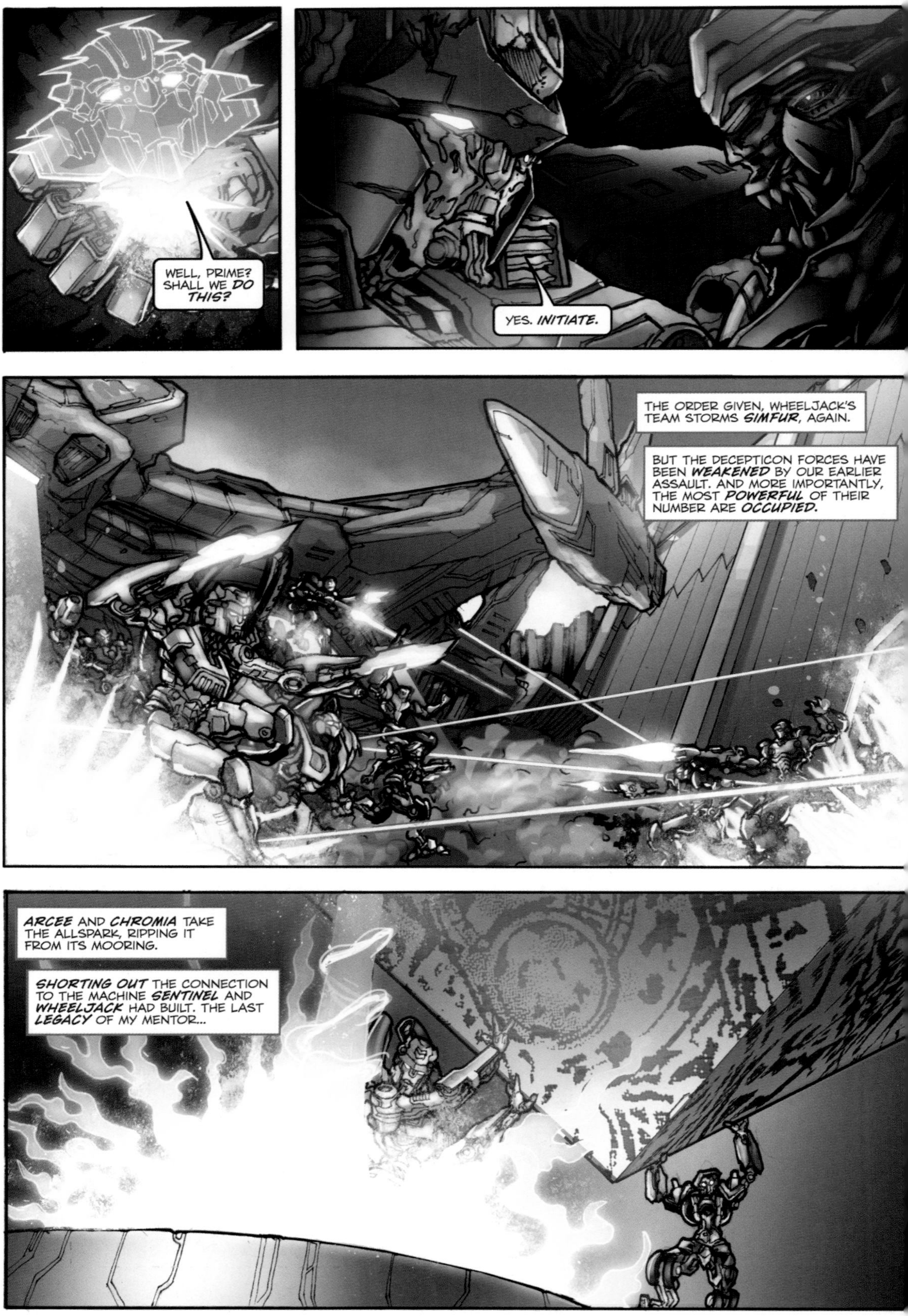
WELL, PRIME? SHALL WE DO THIS?
YES. INITIATE.
THE ORDER GIVEN, WHEELJACK'S TEAM STORMS SIMFUR, AGAIN.
BUT THE DECEPTICON FORCES HAVE BEEN WEAKENED BY OUR EARLIER ASSAULT. AND MORE IMPORTANTLY, THE MOST POWERFUL OF THEIR NUMBER ARE OCCUPIED.
ARCEE AND CHROMIA TAKE THE ALLSPARK, RIPPING IT FROM ITS MOORING.
SHORTING OUT THE CONNECTION TO THE MACHINE SENTINEL AND WHEELJACK HAD BUILT. THE LAST LEGACY OF MY MENTOR...

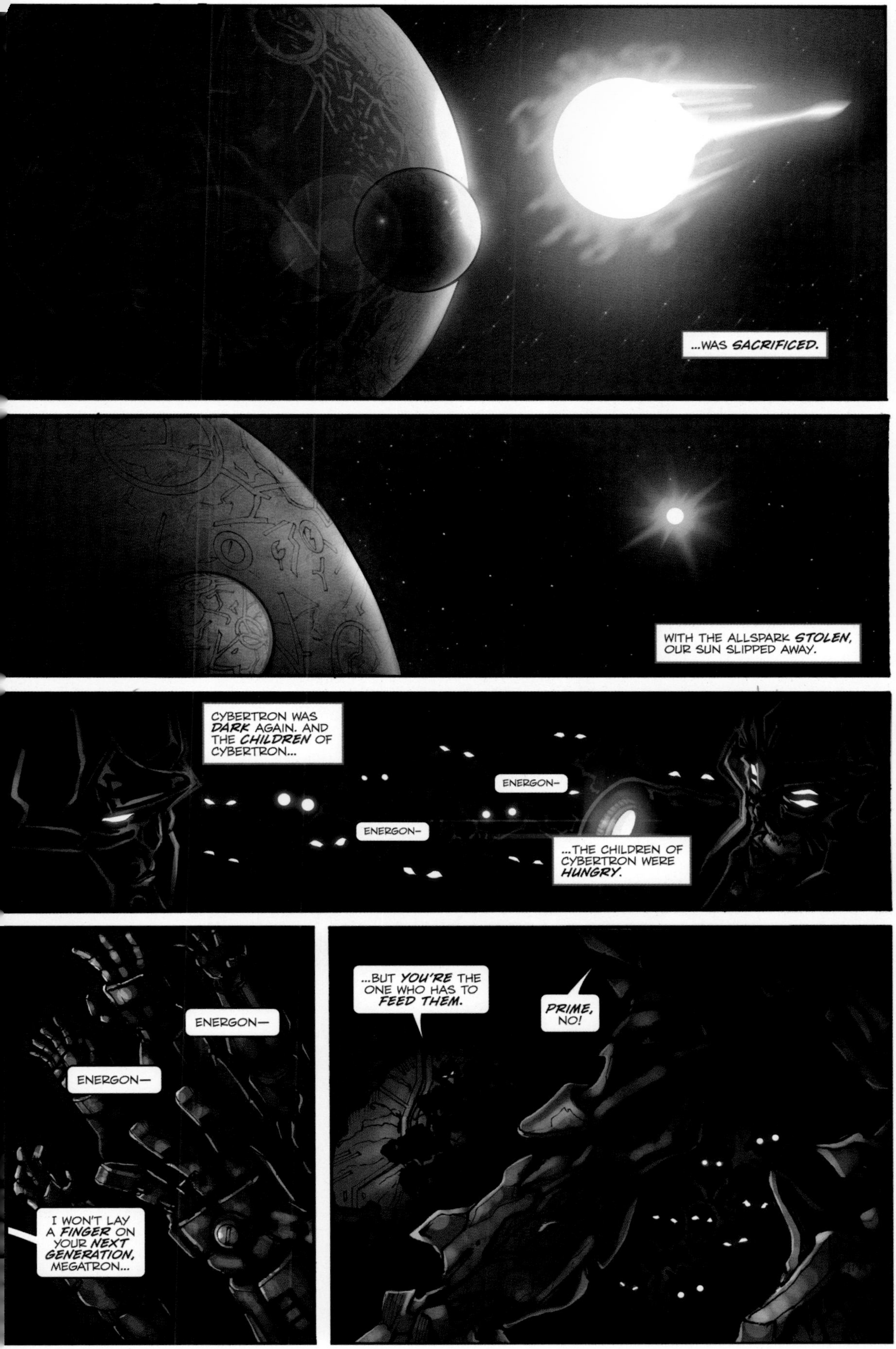
...WAS SACRIFICED.
WITH THE ALLSPARK STOLEN, OUR SUN SLIPPED AWAY.
CYBERTRON WAS DARK AGAIN. AND THE CHILDREN OF CYBERTRON...
ENERGON-
ENERGON-
...THE CHILDREN OF CYBERTRON WERE HUNGRY.
ENERGON—
ENERGON—
I WON'T LAY A FINGER ON YOUR NEXT GENERATION, MEGATRON...
...BUT YOU'RE THE ONE WHO HAS TO FEED THEM.
PRIME, NO!

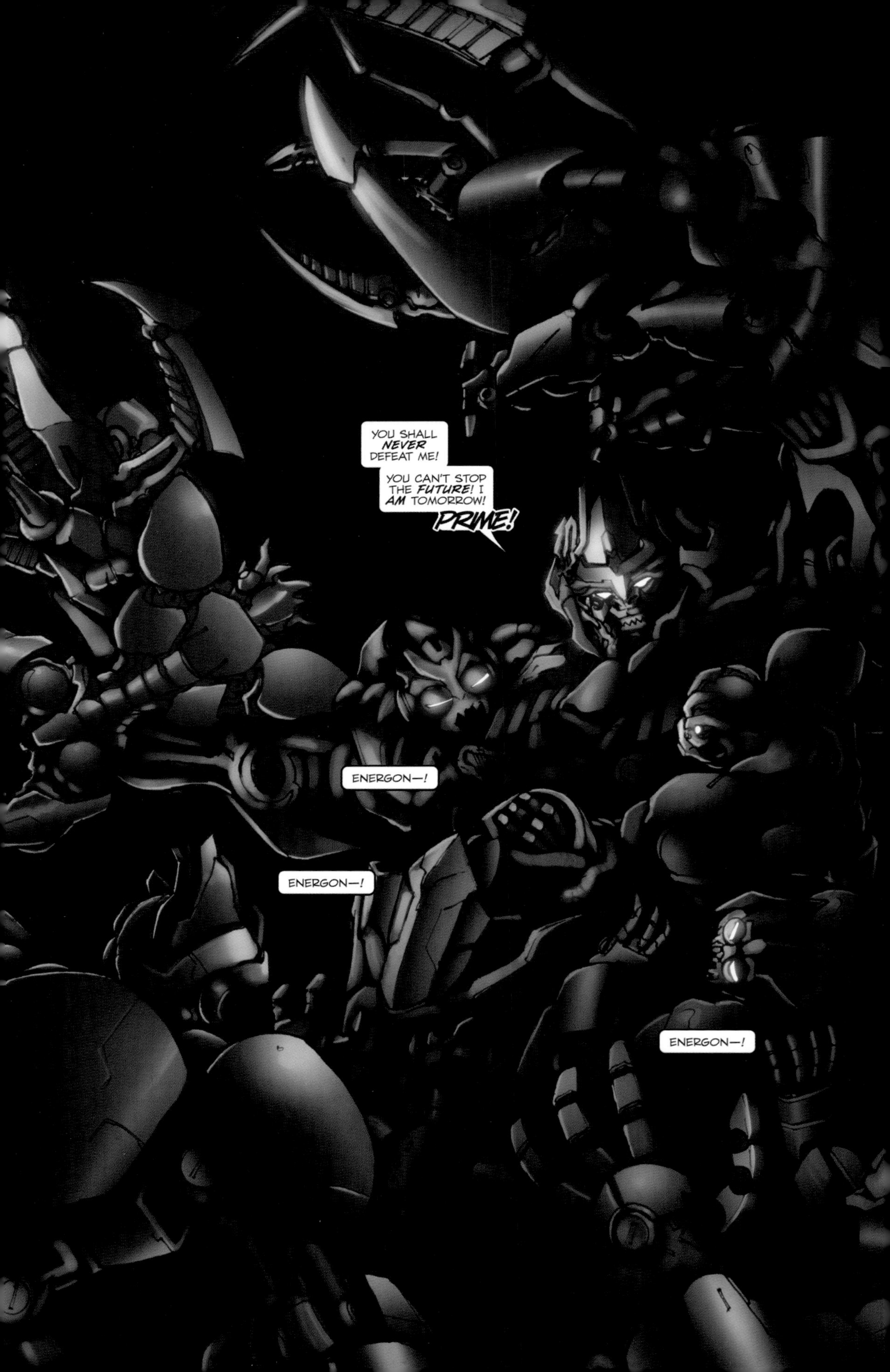
YOU SHALL NEVER DEFEAT ME!
YOU CAN'T STOP THE FUTURE! I AM TOMORROW!
PRIME!
ENERGON—!
ENERGON—!
ENERGON—!

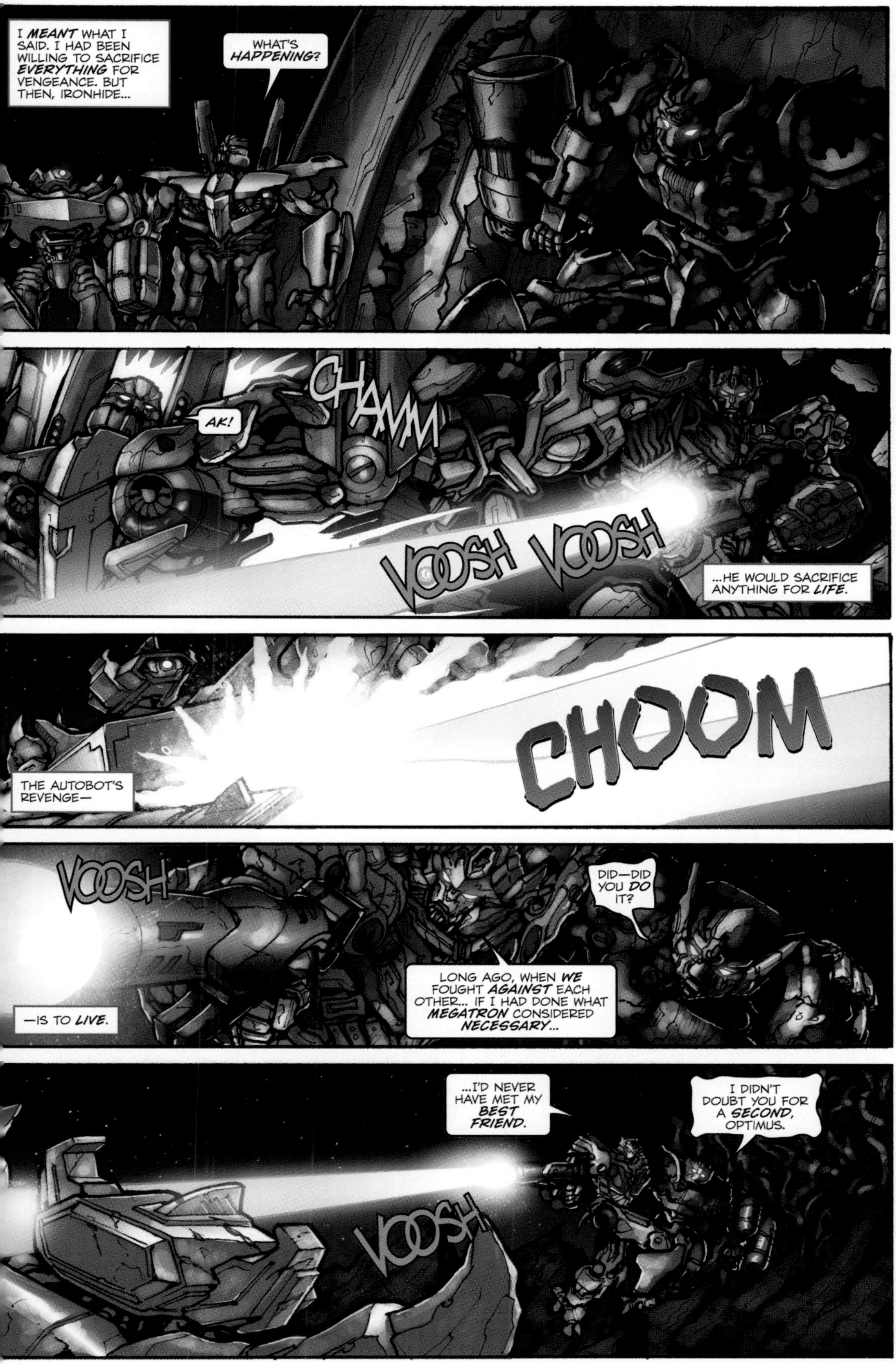
I MEANT WHAT I SAID. I HAD BEEN WILLING TO SACRIFICE EVERYTHING FOR VENGEANCE. BUT THEN, IRONHIDE...
WHAT'S HAPPENING?
CHAMM
AK!
VOOSH VOOSH
...HE WOULD SACRIFICE ANYTHING FOR LIFE.
CHOOM
THE AUTOBOT'S REVENGE—
VOOSH
—IS TO LIVE.
DID—DID YOU DO IT?
LONG AGO, WHEN WE FOUGHT AGAINST EACH OTHER... IF I HAD DONE WHAT MEGATRON CONSIDERED NECESSARY...
...I'D NEVER HAVE MET MY BEST FRIEND.
I DIDN'T DOUBT YOU FOR A SECOND, OPTIMUS.
VOOSH

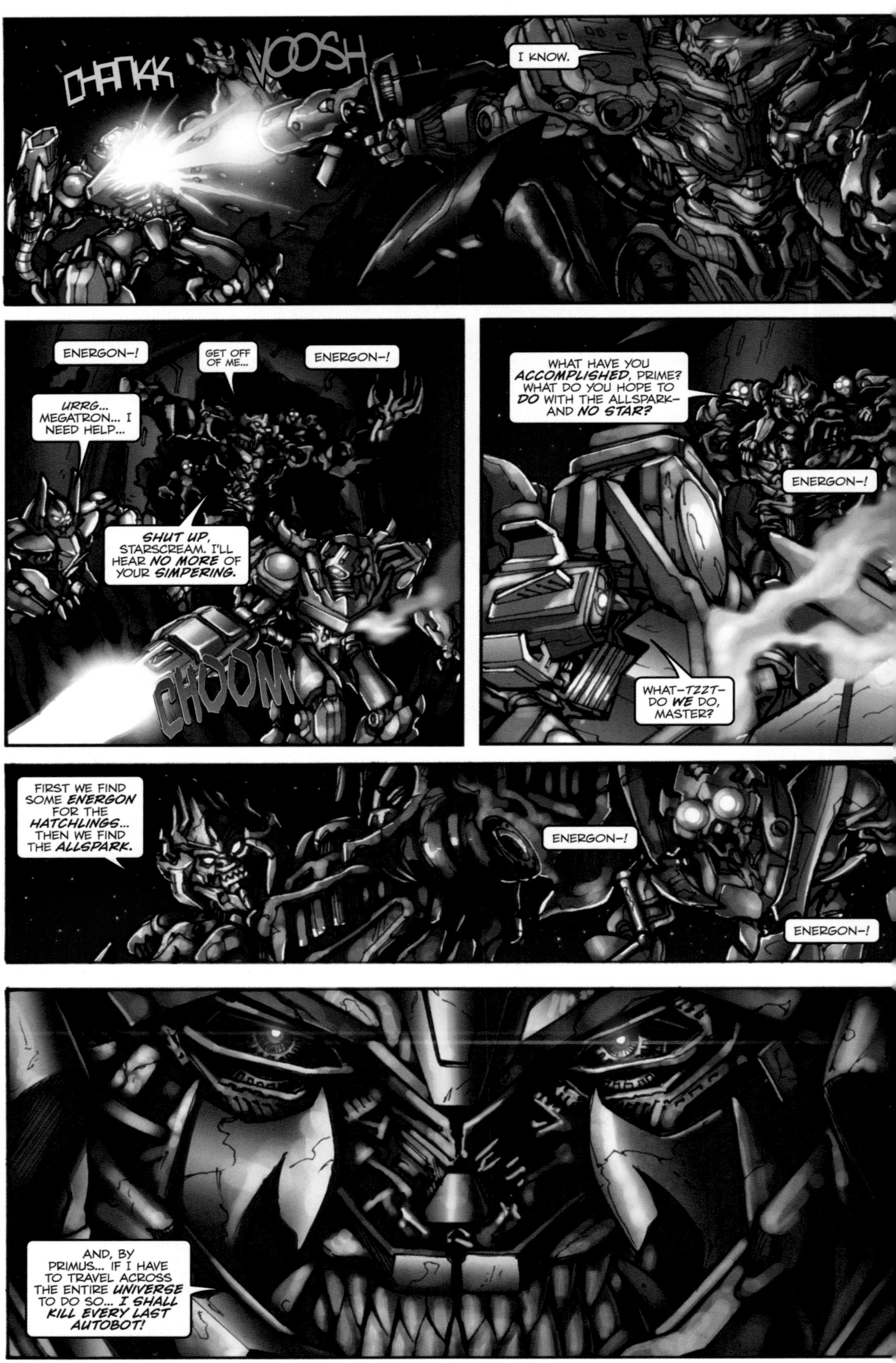
CHANKK
VOOSH
I KNOW.
ENERGON-!
GET OFF OF ME...
ENERGON-!
URRG... MEGATRON... I NEED HELP...
SHUT UP, STARSCREAM. I'LL HEAR NO MORE OF YOUR SIMPERING.
CHOOM
WHAT HAVE YOU ACCOMPLISHED, PRIME? WHAT DO YOU HOPE TO DO WITH THE ALLSPARK-AND NO STAR?
ENERGON-!
WHAT-TZZT-DO WE DO, MASTER?
FIRST WE FIND SOME ENERGON FOR THE HATCHLINGS... THEN WE FIND THE ALLSPARK.
ENERGON-!
ENERGON-!
AND, BY PRIMUS... IF I HAVE TO TRAVEL ACROSS THE ENTIRE UNIVERSE TO DO SO... I SHALL KILL EVERY LAST AUTOBOT!

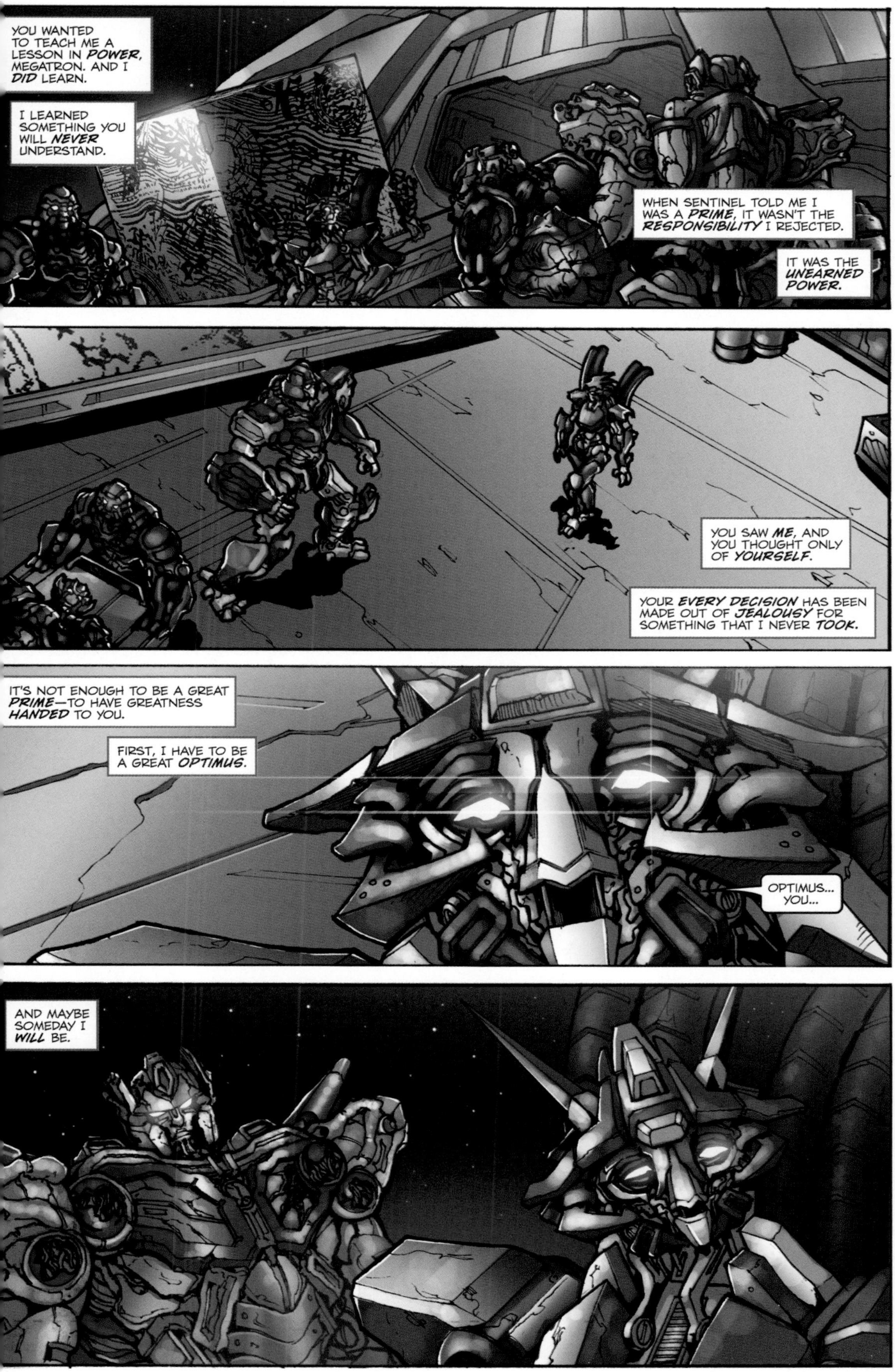
YOU WANTED TO TEACH ME A LESSON IN POWER, MEGATRON. AND I DID LEARN.
I LEARNED SOMETHING YOU WILL NEVER UNDERSTAND.
WHEN SENTINEL TOLD ME I WAS A PRIME, IT WASN'T THE RESPONSIBILITY I REJECTED.
IT WAS THE UNEARNED POWER.
YOU SAW ME, AND YOU THOUGHT ONLY OF YOURSELF.
YOUR EVERY DECISION HAS BEEN MADE OUT OF JEALOUSY FOR SOMETHING THAT I NEVER TOOK.
IT'S NOT ENOUGH TO BE A GREAT PRIME—TO HAVE GREATNESS HANDED TO YOU.
FIRST, I HAVE TO BE A GREAT OPTIMUS.
OPTIMUS... YOU...
AND MAYBE SOMEDAY I WILL BE.

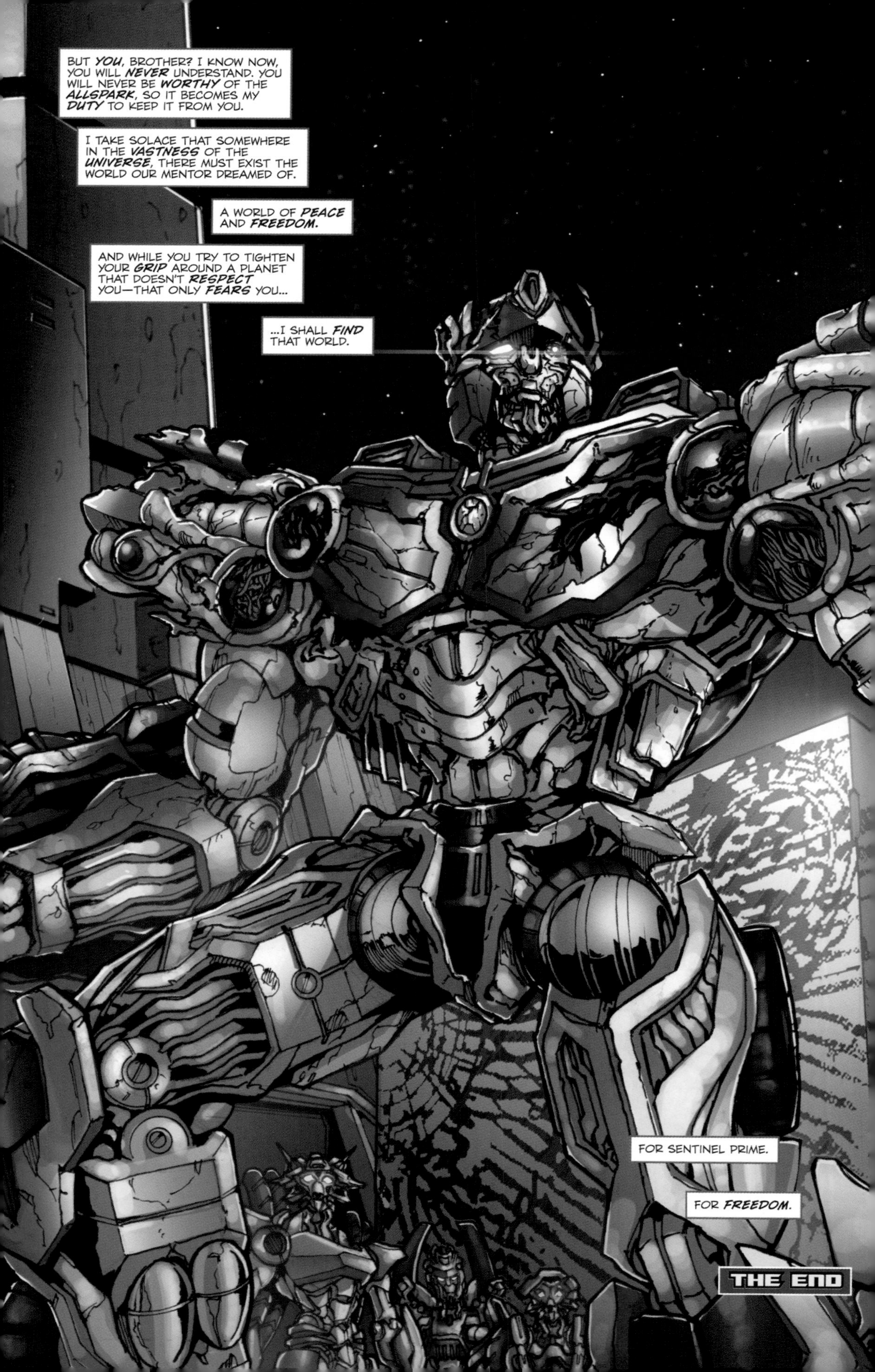
BUT YOU, BROTHER? I KNOW NOW, YOU WILL NEVER UNDERSTAND. YOU WILL NEVER BE WORTHY OF THE ALLSPARK, SO IT BECOMES MY DUTY TO KEEP IT FROM YOU.
I TAKE SOLACE THAT SOMEWHERE IN THE VASTNESS OF THE UNIVERSE, THERE MUST EXIST THE WORLD OUR MENTOR DREAMED OF.
A WORLD OF PEACE AND FREEDOM.
AND WHILE YOU TRY TO TIGHTEN YOUR GRIP AROUND A PLANET THAT DOESN'T RESPECT YOU—THAT ONLY FEARS YOU...
...I SHALL FIND THAT WORLD.
FOR SENTINEL PRIME.
FOR FREEDOM.
THE END